He[barcode]

AND THE GHOST TRAIN

by Christopher Awdry

illustrated by Ken Stott

First published in Great Britain in this edition 1997
Reprinted 1999 by Egmont Children's Books Limited
239 Kensington High Street, London W8 6SA

Britt Allcroft's Thomas the Tank Engine & Friends
Based on The Railway Series by The Rev W Awdry
© Britt Allcroft (Thomas) LLC 1997
THOMAS THE TANK ENGINE & FRIENDS is a trademark of
Britt Allcroft Inc in the USA, Mexico and Canada and of Britt
Allcroft (Thomas) Limited in the rest of the world
THE BRITT ALLCROFT COMPANY is a trademark
of The Britt Allcroft Company plc

ISBN 0 7497 3043 9

5 7 9 10 8 6

Printed in Great Britain

A fair had come to the Island of Sodor. Men had set up stalls and rides near the junction. A notice on one of them said it was a GHOST TRAIN.

At the station everyone was talking about ghosts.
"What is a ghost train?" asked Henry.
"It is a tunnel that trains run through," his driver explained.

"It's full of ghosts and other spooky things."
"I'm not scared of stupid old ghosts," Henry said.
But he did not want to meet one, just in case...

That evening Henry's driver told him: "Part of the tunnel roof has collapsed. The Fat Controller says we must take some men to clear away the rubble."

"Bother," grumbled Henry. "I was looking forward to a rest." Still grumbling, Henry pushed two trucks and a van full of workmen into the tunnel.

He was going nicely when suddenly there was a
loud clanking noise.
"Your tender is off the line," said his driver.

"We must have run into some rubble. We can't go forward and we can't go back. We shall have to wait until the Fat Controller can sort something out."

It was very quiet in the tunnel. The workmen walked home and Henry dozed, but he woke up with a start. He was moving!

"Ooooooooooooh...er!" wailed a ghostly voice and a white shape floated towards him. Henry was terrified. His wheels were shaking but he hurried on.

Then he saw a station ahead. He felt much better now.
He slowed down to stop, but when he saw what was
on the platform he did not want to!

The station had a skeleton staff and a Very Thin Controller.
And waiting to catch the train was a vampire!

When he heard "poooop poooop" in the distance,
Henry felt better.
"That sounds like Gordon," he said.

But it was a ghostly, shadowy Gordon who
rushed towards him with a scream and a roar.

Just as Henry felt he could bear no more,
he heard his driver's voice.

"Wake up, Henry," the driver said.
"Your tender is back on the line. We can go home now."

Henry was delighted. He went quickly back to the shed and had a long drink of water. He felt better after that.

But he was careful not to tell the other engines about the Ghost Train. He was sure they would laugh at him.